Footprints in the Sand

A play

Colin Crowther

Samuel French—London
New York-Toronto-Hollywood

CHARACTERS

Man, over 40
Woman, over 50
Girl, over 15
Old Woman, over 60

NOTE

Directors may wish to know that the play is set in a real place and dramatizes, in part at least, what is known of the life of a real person — the Welsh saint Dwynwen, who lived in the fifth century. Although virtually unknown today outside Wales, she became so popular as the patron saint of lovers that at the Dissolution of the Monasteries, her shrine was the second most popular place of pilgrimage in Wales, after that of St David. The real Dwynwen fell in love with a dissolute Welsh prince called Maelog, ran away when she realized what he was really like, and spent her life as a hermit on Llanddeusant, a tiny island promontory off the south coast of Anglesey, where this play is set. The play came partly out of wondering what Dwynwen would have made of the troops of hopeful pilgrims who made their way to her island retreat, hoping to test the faithfulness of suspect husbands or to persuade young women to marry them ...

The core of the play, though, is not the real life of an ancient Welsh saint, nor even the very real pain of a man facing a terrible and painful future now. This is a play about the ability of people in extreme situations, in any age or place, to find the courage and faith to transform their suffering. So please don't let your actors play it like Greek tragedy on a bad day, and don't let the pace drop to that of a plague dirge! Think instead what you want to share with the audience; a heart-warming and life-affirming tale of real people, then and now, finding the courage to place their footprints in the sand.

Colin and Mary Crowther
March 2001

Other titles by Colin Crowther,
published by Samuel French Ltd

Noah's Ark (*with Mary Crowther*)
Tryst

Exultation is the going
Of an island soul to sea;
Past the houses, past the headlands,
Into deep eternity.

Emily Dickinson

FOOTPRINTS IN THE SAND

A beach. Autumn. Noon

From UR, *sand dunes sweep down to a wide beach of sand and shingle which runs from* UL *to* DR *and then down to the sea* DL. *All this should be very simply suggested. (See the Ground Plan on p. 34) There are three entrances:* UR, DR *and* UL. *The* UR *exit suggests that, off stage, the dunes rise to a little island, jutting out from the shore. The* UL *exit leads back to the mainland. The exit* DR *suggests the beach curves round a sheltered bay*

When the play begins, the cyclorama shows a mackerel sky on a warm September day. In the course of the play the lights change from blue and cream to red and yellow as the light fades to the beginning of sunset. If music is required, then try Vaughan Williams' "Toward the Unknown Region". Otherwise, all we hear are the gentle sounds of surf and seagulls

A Man is standing in the sea, DL, *gazing out to the far horizon, out* L. *(When he moves, he does so hesitantly, holding his left arm limply, for the whole of his left side has been affected by a stroke, but only mildly, and we should not, at first, be aware of this. It is the effect on his mind of an even worse illness that the stroke has triggered which is concerning him and should concern us. He is angry, frightened, bitter, absorbed in his own pain)*

After a pause, a Woman enters UR, *ascending the dunes. She moves very smoothly, never looking where she is placing her feet, but always sure, always steady. She is strong, mysterious, laconic, uncompromising but not uncaring*

The Man does not notice the Woman. She watches him. There is a pause

Woman Have you found it?

The Man glances over his shoulder

What you were looking for. Out there?
Man (*turning back*) No.
Woman Perhaps I can help? (*She stops* R *of* C)
Man No …Thank you.
Woman Two pairs of eyes?
Man Can't help.
Woman Can't?

The Man tries to wade ashore but his feet are stuck

Man (*losing his balance*) I don't need help.

The Woman shrugs

The Man falls over

Woman Quite right. You can help yourself. I'll just — watch.
Man Damn you.
Woman Bless you.

The Man struggles out of the water and into a sitting position on the beach, facing the sea. He begins to rub life back into his calves

There is a pause

Man I'm sorry. I didn't mean damn *you*, just ——
Woman Damn everything?
Man No. Yes.
Woman What brought you here?
Man God knows.

The Woman considers this for a moment. She nods to herself, then steps down the DS *side of the dunes and sits down looking off* R

Woman People rarely come here, now.
Man It's a long walk.
Woman Is it?
Man Too much effort for most people.
Woman Yes. Any sort of effort is too much for most people. But not for you?
Man No.
Woman People need a reason to come here now.

The Man does not rise to the bait. The Woman smiles. She is patient. She enjoys waiting. He will talk when he is ready

The sand, the sea, the sky are not enough. Not any more.

Pause. The Man rises, stiffly

Woman So, most days, I have it to myself.
Man Summer visitors, surely? (*He dusts the sand off his clothes, awkwardly. This is the first time that it is noticeable that he does not use his left hand*)
Woman Summer's over.
Man (*remembering*) September.
Woman My summer.
Man Mine too.

Pause. The Man takes a few steps, unsteadily, towards the sea

The trouble is …
Woman Yes?
Man You can't see anything.
Woman What did you hope to see?
Man I thought it was the city. Too many buildings blocking out the sky, too many people crowding out the silence. I thought maybe

here — somewhere like this place — I could ... see, hear — more
clearly.

Woman (*laughing*) But here the mist blurs the view and the waves
lap in upon your silence.

Man (*turning to the Woman; smiling*) Yes.

Woman And strange women engage you in conversation.

Man Yes.

Woman I could leave you to your ——

Man (*taking a step towards the Woman*) No.

Woman Sure? You have only to say the word.

Man You were here first.

Woman (*seriously*) But *you* are here *now*.

The Man shrugs. During the following he walks US, *along the water-line, still hobbling a little*

Man It's a beautiful place.

The Woman sits, shivering, on the dunes

Woman On a beautiful day.

The Man stops, facing US, *looking left and right*

You could go back. Start again. Somewhere else.

The Man walks towards UR

Man (*pointing off* R) Where does this lead?

Woman Round the island.

Man Is it far?

Woman Five minutes and you're back here again.

The Man reaches UC. *He gives up*

Man Too far.

Woman   It's a very small island — not even that really: a promontory. It used to be further away from the mainland. But over the centuries, the channel silted up, the sand swept in.

The Man moves, slowly, towards C

Man   I can't see anything out there.
Woman   We were never meant to look too far ahead. The future ——

The Man stops

Man   (*sharply*) I know my future. What I need is the courage to face it. Or escape it. (*He turns and starts to walk towards the sea*)
Woman   And that is what you came here to find?
Man   No, I … I don't know. (*He crouches, facing out to sea and fingering the sand*) Three years ago I had a stroke, not a big one, nothing life-threatening. Then another. Now, the blood in my head has begun to leak, dripping tiny drops of blood on to my brain. And every drop … With every drop … I lose — something else. The power to … First it was little things. How to cook my own food, find my way home — I can get out, I just can't get back. Little things. Soon these headaches, this confusion — (*he sits, suddenly and awkwardly*) my balance … I'm drowning — losing my mind!
Woman   And you need the courage to face it.
Man   (*turning to face the Woman, leaning on his right arm*) Face it? Face losing my mind? Face the slow grinding away of my power to think, to speak, to know who I am?
Woman   (*looking beyond him to the seas*) Courage to escape it, then?

The Man follows her gaze, then shrugs

You are alive.
Man   But soon I shall not *know* I am alive. I shall sit there, twitching and gibbering and drooling, not able to feed myself or clean up my

own — mess. (*He struggles up, brushing off the sand*) Not even know I've made a mess. What use is life if I do not know I am alive? Who am I when I no longer know even where or who I am?

Pause

Woman What else?
Man (*jerking upright*) Eh?
Woman What else is there in this future of yours?
Man Isn't that enough?
Woman (*rising*) Oh no. You see the storm clouds, hear the distant thunder. But there is more — to even the darkest storm there is always more.
Man What more?
Woman Something perhaps to help you face it. Or escape it.
Man (*ironically*) Oh? And what is that?
Woman (*breaking to* DRC) Good. You have found your question. Now search. And you will find your answer. Seek and you will find. (*She stops and turns to him*) But be warned, you *will* find your answer.
Man (*turning to face her*) I'm not afraid.
Woman No?

The Man turns away. There is a pause. The Woman heads away back on to the dunes. He tries to think of some way to keep her here

Man Has anyone ever lived here?
Woman A long time ago.
Man How long?
Woman Does it matter?
Man No.
Woman The first was a woman — well, a girl, really. You'd like her. She grew up — over there. (*She points off stage*, UL) At Aberffraw. By winter, she lived on her father's farm. By summer, she stayed at court — for those were the days when the princes of Gwyneth had their summer court at Aberffraw. (*She sits on the dunes, a girl again, her hands clasped round her knees*)

During the following speech the Man becomes fascinated and walks towards the Woman, then kneels on the beach looking up to her

A dark village now, of dull, resentful concrete. Then, a busy, wooden fort: ditch, pallisades, gate — through to a vast square, with stables, kitchens, a carpenter's workshop, blacksmith's forge, granary, foodstores, brewery, laundry — through to the palace, a glowing, pine-gold wooden palace, two storeys high. Below, the stores — meat, corn, oats, ale, mead. Above, up a wide wooden staircase, the Great Hall. On the right, the solar, and another storey where the prince and his family lived, in a square tower, with rushes on the floor, warmed by a charcoal brazier, lit by tallow candles, tapestries around the walls. Hermits praying in stony deserts faced lovers dancing through green meadows: the only choices her young mind could picture, her young fingers could embroider ... Here, a settle for the queen, stools for herself and the other maid-in-waiting. There, the dragon chair of the prince of Gwyneth, dragon's head rearing above it, dragon arms falling, scale over scale, to dragon claws, gripping two great glistening balls of oak — symbol of the palace, high seat of the princes of Gwynedd at Aberffraw.

Man It sounds — magical. (*He turns and makes himself comfortable, a child again, living a bedtime story as he snuggles down, leaning against the dunes*)

Woman It was. The roar of laughter, rumble of argument, ripple of music, rising, sparking, like the smoke from the open fire. (*She rises to her knees*) But through that smoke, through a tiny square window in the solar, she could look down and see them, see the men — stiff-backed freemen, tenant farmers like her father; soldiers, merchants, scholars — see them leaning like hungry dogs to catch a word from the high table of the princes. And at the end — at the far end of that high table — the youngest, prettiest prince leaned back in his chair, bored with men, longing for distraction, idly watching the smoke rise from the fire, up and up to the rafters. Suddenly, his eyes caught a spark, saw reflected in that spark, a face, a tiny, pale face looking down at him through the small square window in the solar.

Man This woman … ?

Woman Dwynwen her name. Maid-in-waiting to the queen. She loved that pretty prince. Maelog, his name. Loved him. With all her hope and heart. (*She shivers and rises*)

Man And he?

Woman They met next morning — almost accidentally — by the stables. (*She walks to the* DS *end of the dunes and puts a foot up on the higher level*) She offered him her heart and pressed on him a tiny posy of violets she'd embroidered. He pressed on her — his body. The posy fell. Violets ground under royal boot. (*She crushes the sand beneath her foot as Maelog once crushed the violets*)

Man I'm sorry.

Woman To her, it was the worst kind of betrayal. To him it was a game, a kind of sport. (*She steps down on to the beach*) She ran. He ran after. Home to her father. But he — good man, kind, safe, silly man — saw only his good fortune. Told her to brush her hair and smile on the young prince. In the end …

Man She killed herself.

Woman Women are not so foolish.

Man I only meant ——

Woman (*moving to the sea* DC) Men, like trees, stand proud — upright, defiant, daring life's storms to do their worst. And when they do — when winds blow and ice cracks — then trees fall, split, die, still wondering "Why me?" Women, like the sea grass that clings precariously to these dunes — whipped by wind and blistered by salt water, scorched by sun, walked all over by men and crushed by their unthinking children — women, like the sea grass, bend and sway. Survive and thrive.

Man (*crushed*) I'm sorry.

The Woman turns back to the sea, satisfied; during the following she walks along the water's edge, from DC *to the extreme* LC

Woman She kept on running — walking — limping — till one fine September day she reached here. The outermost fringe of land. As

far from human habitation — from unfaithful men — as far from
their deceitful ways as she could reach.

Man And he?

Woman Gave up the chase. Too much effort. Maelog turned his
pretty face to more willing prey.

Man I know how she felt.

Woman Angry, bitter, betrayed ——

Man Frightened?

*The Woman, now LC, nods, then faces off stage, out to sea. There is
a pause*

Who lives here now?

Woman No-one.

Man Then — who are you?

Woman Driftwood. (*She turns to look at him*) Who are you?

Man Does it matter?

Woman No.

Man I wish I'd met her.

Woman (*casually*) Then you shall. (*She turns away to look out to
sea*)

The Man rises

Man Is this a dream?

Woman No.

Man Ah, I see.

Woman No, you don't.

Man It's happened, hasn't it? It's begun. The madness?

Woman Not yet.

The Man leans back against the dunes

Man Then — am I …?

Woman Walk.

Man What?

Woman Walk. Keep your blood flowing.

Man My blood flows. Blood flowing is not my problem. (*But anyway he obeys her. He reaches* C *and pauses*) What happened to her?

Woman (*very offhandedly*) To Dwynwen? See for yourself.

Man But surely ——? (*He takes a step towards the Woman*)

The Girl enters UL, *clearly distressed. She has wet hair*

The Girl runs C, *passing so close to the Man that he whirls round. He sinks back against the dunes*

Old Woman (*off*) Dwynwen! Dwynwen!

Girl No! No!

The Man reaches out a hand to touch the Girl, to see if she is real

Man She's so young.

The Old Woman enters UL, *breathless, exhausted. She heads* C

N.B. Until the last moments of the play, neither the Girl nor the Old Woman looks at nor acknowledges the presence of either the Man or the Woman

Old Woman Child, wait!

Girl Leave me alone!

Old Woman There's nowhere left to run.

The Girl runs, desperately, to RC

Only the sea.

Girl Then I shall throw myself into the sea!

Man Poor girl.

Old Woman Child!

Girl How could he? Nana, how could he?

The Old Woman stops, quite close to the Man — but she cannot see him

Old Woman That's men for you.

Man No, it's not.

Girl (*stepping past the Man*) No, it's not.

Old Woman Some men. (*She moves slightly* US *of the Man*)

Girl Oh, Nana! (*She sinks to her knees in despair*)

Old Woman Their nature — when the heat is on them — like stags.

Girl I've never seen a stag.

Old Woman (*moving to the Girl*) Beautiful creatures.

Girl Nana, he could have had my heart!

Old Woman (*going down on one knee and putting an arm round the Girl*) I know, I know.

Man (*rising and addressing the Woman*) Can she see me?

Woman No.

Man Hear me?

Old Woman Come back with me. Your father will ——

Girl (*rising angrily and breaking to the sea* DC) My father! I went to him for safety. He betrayed me!

Old Woman He's sorry now. Worried for you.

Girl No, he's not.

The Old Woman struggles to her feet

Old Woman He will be. Please, Dwynwen, come back with me. The prince — your father ——

Girl No. (*She turns* US, *facing the Woman whom she cannot see*)

The Woman gazes intently at the Girl

Old Woman They are our masters. We must obey them.

Woman ⎤
Girl   ⎦ (*together*) No!

The Old Woman moves C

Old Woman If they do wrong, 'tis on their heads and on their souls. If we disobey them, 'tis on ours.

Man No!

Girl No!

Pause. The Girl turns away towards the sea. The Old Woman thinks up a new approach

Old Woman You are a woman now. One day you'll marry — have to marry — what else is there? — and it will be at your father's choosing. Then you'll do your husband's bidding. Till then you are your father's and must obey him.

Man That's not fair.

Girl (*breaking* DR) It isn't fair.

Old Woman What has fair to do with anything? You're a woman, a daughter of Eve, and for her sins you suffer. Now rise, do as you're told, and return with me. (*She takes a step towards the Girl*)

Man Poor girl, poor girl.

Old Woman See sense, girl. We'll not be home by nightfall as it is. Come away!

Girl (*turning to face the Old Woman, her mind made up*) I'm staying here.

Man Good for you!

Old Woman Here? There's nothing here but sand and sea! You'll perish.

Girl Then I'll perish.

Old Woman And what of me? If I go back without you? He'll beat me senseless.

Girl You tried your best.

Old Woman And when has that ever counted with him? (*She turns* US *and faces* UL)

Man I didn't realize.

Woman (*taking a few steps* UL) Every decision has its consequence. Every pebble its ripple.

The Old Woman turns to face off R. *She is, of course, looking straight into the face of the Woman, but still cannot see her. The Woman looks at her closely*

Old Woman Since your mother died I've had the rearing of you, though I am only a bond-servant and you are the daughter of a fine farmer. Now you're raised and gone — gone mad — and all my work's undone. Any hope I had of quiet and ease in my age is gone. He'll turn me out. I'll be a beggar. Worse. Dwynwen, for my sake, come back with me.

Girl I'm sorry.

Man Perhaps ——

Old Woman (*turning to face the Girl*) I never told you this before. When my father sold me — to pay off his debts to his landlord, your father — I was but twelve. That same night, your father — took me.

Man Oh, God!

Old Woman His right, I know. But ——

Girl Oh, Nana!

The Woman comes and puts her arm round the Old Woman's shoulder. The Old Woman seems to draw some comfort from that

Woman I had no choice. And nor have you, Dwynwen. (*She takes a step towards the Girl*) You can run and run, Dwynwen, but you'll not find it. In the end we all need something to eat and somewhere to sleep, someone to call friend and some place to call home. In the end we all come home, and when you do, Dwynwen, I'll be there.

The Old Woman exits UL

The Woman turns to watch the Old Woman go. The Girl suddenly runs C *as if to call the Old Woman back. The Woman spins round to face her. The Man misses all of this and just stands up stiffly and turns away* DS

Man She can go now.

The Girl despairs. She turns towards the sea

Woman You wanted to see her.

Man I've seen enough. Her problem is not my problem.

Woman (*taking a step towards the Man*) She is in pain.

The Girl sinks to her knees

Man (*roaring*) So am I!

Woman Perhaps she can help you.

Man (*taking a step towards the Woman*) My pain is mine. There is no pain in this world like my pain!

Woman Except the pain of those who love you and can only watch you suffer.

Man (*turning away*) It does not help to know that others too have suffered.

Woman (*taking another step towards him*) But it does help to know they have suffered and found meaning.

Man The lover or the hermit.

Woman Her choice.

Man (*taking a step towards the Girl*) In the end, I suppose, we all have to choose.

Woman You can help her make that choice. To go on or give up. Face life or escape it.

The Girl struggles to her feet and starts to wade out into the sea

Man No.

Girl I can't go on.

Man You must. (*He rushes to the Woman*) Stop her!

Woman I can't. No one can. If she's determined. (*She walks away* UC)

The Man rushes into the waves, to the seaward side of the Girl. Still she cannot see him. He is just a voice in her head

Man You have your life before you.

Girl (*turning away to face* DC) Behind me. It's over.

Man (*desperately*) No. It's not … You're young … You— (*To the Woman*) Help me!

Woman How?

The Man wades to the shore

Man Stop me talking platitudes!
Woman Then stop thinking of yourself and start thinking of her!

The Man walks down the shoreline towards the Girl

Girl I can't stay. Not here.
Man You could go back.

The Girl breaks further DS, *still in the sea*

Girl No!
Man You could stay here.
Girl It won't work.
Man Make it work.
Girl How can it? Nana was right. There is nothing here. Nothing
  to eat, nowhere to sleep, no food, no shelter. (*She wades ashore*)
Man Then make some. Turn this — wilderness into — a — garden.
Girl It's raining. (*This is the final straw. She droops*)
Man You need shelter.
Girl There is no shelter!
Man Then make some. Try!
Girl I don't want to try. Not anymore.
Man (*quietly*) Then what do you want, Dwynwen?
Girl I want to die! (*She sinks to her knees*)
Man (*to the Woman, pleading*) Give me the words! Help me!
Woman (*mounting the* US *side of the dunes*) You *have* the words.
  Deep down we all have those words we need to speak, those
  words we need to hear.

The Man kneels behind the Girl, to her R

Man (*quietly, realizing it as he speaks*) No life is ever over. In your
  body or out of your body, *you* go on.
Girl (*rising*) What good can come of this — of all this mess and pain
  and … ?

Man The future is not ours to know.
Girl Then what? (*She breaks* DR)
Man The present. We have only our present.

The Girl breaks DC

Girl I cannot see it.
Man Not on the far horizon. Here. Beneath your feet. (*He scoops up a handful of sand*)
Girl Nothing but sand and shingle!

The Girl exits, running, DR, *kicking the sand*

Man (*shouting after her*) And shells. (*He finds one in his hands and holds it up. Then he speaks quietly, puzzling over what he could possibly mean*) You'll be amazed what can be contained in a single shell. (*He stares after the Girl, and stands up, thrilled at his own achievement*) I found it! I found the words!
Woman Yes.
Man (*turning to the Woman*) Who are you?
Woman A piece of driftwood, twisted by the sea.
Man I can go home now. (*He heads* DR, *marching confidently*)
Woman You can't. Nor can she.
Man But ——?
Woman You brought her back. You told her she could not escape her fate. That she must face it. Now tell her how.

The Man takes a step toward the dunes

The Girl enters suddenly from UR, *her hair awry. She runs up on to the dunes, sways, half jumps and half falls down on to the sand*

Girl I'm so hungry!
Man Haven't I got enough to bear? Don't you understand? Here. (*He pounds his head*) Up here, I'm drowning — drowning in my own blood!

Woman (*dismissively*) One day. Today she is drowning in her own sorrow. And hungry. What is your pain tomorrow compared with her pain today?

Girl So hungry! (*During the following, she scrabbles about in the sand,* C, *feverishly searching for something to eat. She is clearly on the verge of delirium*)

Man Why me?

The Woman walks to the C *of the dunes*

Woman Why you? With all your doctors and medicines and care and shelter? Why not you? Why a man a thousand — fifteen hundred years ago, with none of these? Why should that same illness happen to him? Why a woman, a thousand miles from you, with no medicine, no care, no shelter? Why should it happen to her?

Man All right. (*He turns away from the Woman and sees the Girl more clearly*)

Woman Why you? Why not you.

Girl I shall go mad! (*She lies down, too weak to move, and slowly curls up into a ball, half asleep, half awake through the ensuing dialogue*)

Man Can't I help her — some way — help her? (*He circles above the Girl*)

Woman How?

Man Feed her?

· **Woman** Hands do not stretch so far through time.

The Man breaks to the C, *below the dunes*

Man There must be some way?

Woman She's hungry. Cold. Wet. Lonely. Because she chose to live.

Man I feel — responsible.

Woman You are. We all are. You for her. She for you. Every pebble ripples through time and space. Sins of the father, blessings of the mother — ripple through time and space.

Girl (*whimpering in her fevered sleep*) Frightened. Nana! Help me.
Don't leave me. Nana! (*She tosses about deliriously during the
following*)
Man Oh God. Call her back. (*He runs* UL *and gestures off*) The old
woman! Can't you ——
Woman No. (*She softens*) I can't. (*She moves to the* DS *end of the
dunes*)
Man Why not?
Woman She is not here to call. There is no-one here to call.
Man Can't you help her?
Woman (*turning on the Man*) Can't you?

The Man begins to stagger back to RC, *clutching his head, his
balance badly affected now*

Man This is a dream.
Woman Yours is not the only voice crying in the wind.
Man This is a nightmare!
Woman Yes. But hers. Not yours.

*The Man stops. He and the Woman look at each other; then the Man
turns to the Girl. He has no strength left. He leans against the dunes.
The Woman hums a lullaby, looking down on the Girl*

Man It's like I've got bits of a jigsaw. But no picture to guide me.
Just odd bits of blue. Sky, perhaps, or sea. But no distinguishing
feature. No bird or fish. Not even a cloud or wave. Just blue. (*He
sits, listening to the lullaby*) And no corner bits. Only one straight
edge. Just odd bits of blue. So I can't see how it's meant to look.
Woman Then let me show you infinity. Or at least, the thousand
years of it that I have known.

*The Woman moves behind the Man on the dunes, then kneels and
catches his shoulders, forcing him to look out to the far horizon,
out* L

There is only sand, pressed into rock, hewn into stone, pounded
into pebble, washed into shingle, blown into sand. We are dust,

compacted into bone, strapped into sinew, rising only to fall, tumbling into bone, crumbling into dust. Time and tide washing all away.

Man Then why struggle to stand?

Woman (*rising*) Because we can.

Man (*after a slight pause*) I don't think I can make it on my own.

Woman Every pebble ripples … (*She turns* US)

Pause. The Man moves, unwillingly, helplessly, closer to the Girl

Man Poor girl. She's been through so much.

Woman You will go through worse.

Man That's tomorrow. This is today.

The Woman smiles at the Man and goes back to humming her lullaby

How is she?

During the following speech, the Girl opens out and crawls to the spot of sand just below the Man

Woman Winter has past. The sea has whipped away her anger. The wind has frozen out her pride and the sand has worn away her fear. Spring has come. Now she can begin to take up her life again.

The Man kneels R of the Girl, US *of her, his hands held helplessly out to his side, as if wanting to hold her and knowing that he can't*

Man There's nothing left of her. (*He rises*)

Woman *She* is left. Winter has ground her away till *only* she is left. And again, it's raining. Spring rain.

Man I do not feel it. (*He takes a step towards the sea*)

Woman She does. Her spring — your autumn, remember?

The Girl sits up, looks round, then curls up in a sad little ball, facing out front, DL

Man What is she thinking?
Woman You know what she is thinking.

The Girl begins scrabbling about on the beach, madly searching

Man She wants to find a shell big enough to crawl inside and
    hide ——
Woman And you?
Man — to hide until the storm passes over —— (*He searches in
    the shells at his feet*)
Man If only I could find a shell big enough.
Woman You can't destroy your life and you can't hide from it. You
    have to live it.
Man If only I could tell her ——
Woman Try.

The Man kneels

Man Tide will rise. Tide will fall.

The Girl stops her wild scrabbling

But I will not leave you while you need me. I do not know your
answer but I do know you will find it.

*The Girl relaxes and looks up, perhaps even swaying a little, during
the following*

You will rise up and live again. As sure as tide will rise and tide
will fall.
Woman Raining hard now.

*The Girl finds a shell and holds it up. She wipes the wet hair out of
her eyes, then stands up, hope shining in her eyes*

Girl Lord, I am just a tiny shell on the vast shore of your great ocean.
Fill me. Then pour me out on all these broken shells. (*She steps
forward, facing out* R)

The rain fills the shell; the Girl drinks, exalted. The Man sits back on his haunches and watches, amazed. The Girl rises and moves US, dancing in a huge circle round the stage

The Old Woman enters DR and watches

The Girl does not notice the Old Woman for a while

Old Woman You'll be talking to yourself next.
Girl I don't need to. I talk to the birds and the rabbits and the wind and the sea. (*During the following she dances through the waves, behind the Man, and eventually back to DRC*)

The Old Woman comes to DRC, watching

Old Woman You're alive, then.
Girl Oh, Nana, I'm more alive than I have ever been!
Old Woman You look more dead than alive to me. Girl, what have you been eating?
Girl Eggs, berries, fish thrown up by the winter storms, crabs, mussels, roots, nuts.

The Old Woman steps further towards C

Old Woman You've not lived all winter on roots and fish — like a — a wild thing?

The Girl stops

Girl I have been hungry. But, Nana, I've made it.
Old Woman And where've you lived? In that rough shelter over the dunes?

The Girl nods

Girl I made it myself.
Old Woman I can see.

Girl Sticks dug deep, then twigs plaited through, then mud and turf.
Old Woman Regular palace. And you've slept — on what?
Girl Bracken.
Old Woman My poor girl. (*She holds out her arms*)

The Girl runs into the Old Woman's arms

Girl It's good to see you, Nana. But I'm no one's poor girl now. I've made it, Nana. Cold and wet and hungry, yes. In despair so many times, lonely most times, out of my mind sometimes, but I've made it.

The Girl brings the Old Woman to the dunes and sits her down. The Man, still kneeling C, *turns to watch them*

Old Woman Oh well, you won't be interested in what I've brought you, then.
Girl What?
Old Woman Fresh bread.
Girl Oh, Nana!
Old Woman Soup.
Girl Oh!

The Girl dances on the spot. During the following the Woman moves, to the DS *end of the dunes*

Old Woman Warm blankets and some proper withies to make a decent shelter. And a fire stone.

The Girl stops dancing

Girl (*ecstatic*) Fire! At last!

The Old Woman rises

Old Woman You've ate them things raw? Stayed through this winter with no fire? Lord, girl. (*She pauses, embarrassed, then sits*) Got a brazier, too. Of sorts. And a goat.

Girl (*clapping her hands and dancing around*) Milk!

The Woman sits on the DS *edge of the dunes, laughing silently*

Old Woman Two chickens that are past laying. Or so he thinks.

The Girl dances UC

> And a flagon of mead. A comb of honey — gone a bit dry now.
> A sack of vegetables.

The Girl stops. She goes rigid, suspecting a trap

Girl Who from?
Old Woman Your father.
Girl I'll not go back.
Old Woman All winter long we've thought of you and talked of
you — on our farm and every farm around. In every storm we've
sat up, worrying for you. Not a woman in the village but said a
prayer for you. Soon as winter broke, your father said, "Take these
to her".
Girl But why? (*She returns to the dunes*)
Old Woman Don't you know nothing, girl? It's what men do. Heap
gifts on you. When they want to say sorry. Or please. Or anything
else that sticks in their craw.

The Girl sits on the US *slope of the dunes*

Girl He gave all these?
Old Woman Well he said, Take what you need. (He wasn't too
precise, so nor was I.) But he was feeling generous so I took him
at his word. We called at every house and hut along the way,
thinking you'd be sheltering with some kind soul. But oh, no —
not you! Of course, when they heard your story, they loaded us
with gifts, made us promise we'd call back and tell them how you
were. So, we got a cheese here, oatcakes there, eggs from one
belle-dame and mittens from another, a knife, an axe, and a real

good cooking pot … I'd forgotten that — don't know how … My
brain ——

Girl Nana — how could you carry all that — this far?

Old Woman I couldn't. So I said, "I'm a poor old woman, you can't
expect me to go traipsing through fell and forest on my own." So
he gave me that old cart. Said you could keep it. Aled fixed it. And
I said, "You can't expect him to pull it." So he lent me the mule
— and Aled — to make sure at least he got his mule back.

*The Girl scrambles up on to the higher level then runs down again,
jumping and looking off* R, *trying to get a view over the dunes*

Girl Where is it?

Old Woman You remember Aled's girl? Clumsy lummox but a
good heart? She's unloading it all right now.

Girl Anything else? (*She rushes back*)

Old Woman (*counting the points off on her fingers*) He says he
understands. He was wrong. You were right. Come back or stay
here, the choice is yours. But you're still his daughter, he'll not see
you starve. And one other thing he sent you.

Girl Well?

Old Woman Me.

Girl Nana?

Old Woman Not much of a gift.

Girl The best gift of all. (*She kneels and throws her arms round the
Old Woman*)

Old Woman I don't work — properly — now.

Girl I'll do the work.

Old Woman Not what I mean. This winter — December it was —
something went — wrong — in my head. Been going wrong for
a while. Talking to myself, getting in a rut with words and not
getting out of it, just churning, round and round, like a wheel in
the mud. Then woke up one morning, only didn't. Couldn't talk
right. Getting better now. But it's left me slow. In the head. I can
see things but I don't work out what to do about it till I've dropped
it or spilt it.

Man (*recognizing these symptoms*) Or what it is keeps going round and round in my head. (*He turns and faces out front*)

Old Woman (*carrying on as if there had been no interruption*) Churning round, hour after hour, like a wheel in the mud. Still can't use this arm. And I go ——

Man —— blank. Think you've said something. Find you haven't. People ask and I can't remember if I've answered. And these headaches.

Old Woman Some days better than others.

Man Some days worse.

Old Woman Happens to oldies.

Man And not so oldies. Oh, Nana.

The Girl rises, clearly afraid of mental illness. She turns US

Old Woman Come in threes, they say.

Man Old wives' tale.

Old Woman Most things are.

Man True.

Old Woman The first one takes just bits away, and other tiny blighters nibble away at what's rest — like mice, in your head, little mice eating their way through the best bits and spilling the rest, spilling all those words and ways I used to know — spilling and spoiling them. Spilling and ——

The Man rises, facing out front

Man (*inside his own torment*) It isn't doing, feeling, even thinking that makes you human. It's *knowing* that you're *doing* it. That *I'm* doing it. (*He turns and stumbles* US *during the following*)

Old Woman —— spoiling and spilling. Then comes number two, they say, and they put you in the corner by the fire and you just sits there, dribblin', till they notice the smell, like a baby, only babies is pretty. Then they put you outside. In the barn. With the mice. Spoiling and spilling …

The Man turns to face DS

Man (*in agony*) I am not me if I do not know I am not me!

The Old Woman rises and moves closer to C

Old Woman Then comes number three. Not so bad, number three,
'cos you've caught a chill — well, you would, left outside in the
cold and wet. A mercy really. Anyway, you can't eat by then, so
you goes in a day or two. No, I don't fear number three, it's
number two I fear.

The Man stumbles further DS, *coming virtually face to face with the
Old Woman, during the following. The Old Woman cannot see him*

Man I am lost — to myself — lost in the whole wide world … A
broken shell, on a shingle shore of the world's vast ocean, so
smashed and splintered not even her God could find me!

The Woman rises, helpless, confused. The Girl turns

Girl (*to the Old Woman*) God who made us, he can reach us, even
when we cannot reach ourselves.
Man (*looking at the Old Woman*) How?
Old Woman How?

*The Girl jumps down from the dunes and runs between the Old
Woman and the Man*

Girl Through each other, Nana. Oh Nana, I won't put you out. I'll
be here for when you can talk.
Man And I for when you can't.
Old Woman Won't be enough, child. (*She breaks towards* DR) Oh,
I thank you, but no one can know the sad loneliness of a body that
won't obey you and the awful emptiness of a mind that won't
speak to you, won't listen to what you're telling and telling it to
do!
Man I know. I live that too.

The Girl helps the Old Woman to sit back on the dunes and places herself DS of her, sitting just below the Woman

Woman Then tell her.
Man Me?
Woman No-one else can. No one else knows that terror here.

The Man sits at the Old Woman's feet

Man There is no hurt, no loss, no ache of heart or vacancy of mind, no withering of hope, no canker of the soul, no path of pain — no path at all — however dark or strange or fearsome we will not walk beside you. As sure as tide will rise and tide will fall.

The Woman stands behind the Man and holds out her arms as in a blessing

Woman And there you have it.
Man What?
Woman Your answer.

The Woman turns and walks halfway along the dunes

Old Woman (*comforted*) As sure as tide will rise and tide will fall…
Girl Those words! (*She jumps up and breaks slightly DR*) I heard this voice. In my head. Not my voice. Another, gentle voice. "Tide will rise. Tide will fall. You will find your answer. As sure as tide will rise and tide will fall."
Old Woman Fever.
Girl Yes. In my fever. (*She breaks DRC*) "No life is ever over. In your body or out of your body, *you* go on."
Old Woman Well, you and your voices and me and mine, we'll keep each other merry company!

The Old Woman rises. The Girl helps her

Girl Nothing we can't face together, Nana, nothing we can't face.

Old Woman I'd better go and see where Aled's girl is up to with that unpacking. Daft lummox! (*She moves below the Girl to* DRC. *She looks up, over the dunes, then stops and turns*) There's a fair bit of land on the far side of those dunes.

Girl Yes, I thought perhaps a small field.

Old Woman Mm. I'll get Aled to drive stakes in and then we can plait some branches, keep out the sand and some of this dreadful wind. Plenty of leaf-mould in the forest; that should get the soil going. Maybe plant some vegetables, come the warmer weather.

The Woman stands behind the Girl

Girl
Woman } (*together*) Bless you, Nana.

The Woman and the Girl both shiver. The Woman turns away and walks to US *of the dunes*

Old Woman Bless you, she says! Here, take this. (*She offers the Girl her cloak*) I suppose you'll be building a church next.

Girl A chapel, I thought.

The Old Woman mounts the DS *rise of the dunes, looking off* R

Old Woman Good place for it, up on that headland.

Girl Yes.

The Girl sits on the DS *rise and searches casually through the shells at her feet. Quite suddenly, the Man sits, slightly to* L *of* C, *crosslegged, facing out to sea, supporting his head in his right hand. We should have no reason at this point to suppose that anything is wrong*

Old Woman You'll need stone for that. I'll get Aled, on his way home, to tell them to bring stones.

Girl Tell who?

Old Woman Your neighbours.

Girl Neighbours?

Old Woman I told you, quite a curiosity you've become. All the women feel for you and all the men are — well, half and half, the way men are. Anyway, they'll be coming out to see you, come summer. I'll tell them to bring a stone each. Soon have a little chapel that way.

Girl What do they want to see me for?

Old Woman 'Cos you had the courage to say no, child, to stand up for what is right and good and true. And there's few — men or women will do that. And it's made the men think why they push women around. And the women, why they let them ... (*She moves down to beach level*) So there'll be womenfolk wanting to talk of the problems they're having with their menfolk and the menfolk will come along to carry the stones and help to build your chapel ('cos they won't trust a woman to know how to do it on her own) and they'll stay on, will some of them, to say they don't know how women'd manage at all without their men and then they'll *er* and *umpf*, the way men do, and ask you to take their wives and daughters, and ask what you would do with a woman who would do this and wouldn't do that. Now, a woman who could stand there in the middle of that sort of storm, guiding the two of them safely ashore, such a woman could do a mighty power of good in this or any place. In this or any time. (*She continues on her way* DR)

Girl You could do that, Nana.

Old Woman No, I can't listen without butting in — never could. Can't talk without taking sides. Can't do something right without crowing about it. But you can. And I can sit in that hut we're going to build and tend the fire and stir the soup. Which reminds me...

The Old Woman exits DR

The Girl cherishes her special shell

Man (*still facing out to sea*) And did she?

The Woman moves behind the Girl

Woman As winter turned to summer, as youth gave way to age. *We* stayed.

The Girl rises, holding up her shell, looking off, DL

And the lovers came and the legend grew and the stones came and the chapel grew. And on the altar in the chapel at Llanddeusant stood — for all to see and puzzle at ——

The Girl turns to face the dunes. The Woman closes the Girl's hands on the shell and smiles down at her

— a single — shell.

The Girl turns, exalted, and runs off DR

The Woman moves to the C *of the dunes*

Woman You have your answer. Now live it.
Man (*rubbing his right hand across his head*) How ——?

The Old Woman and the Girl enter UR, *both strong, both seeing the Man now*

Old Woman There is no hurt, no loss, no ache of heart or vacancy of mind …

The Old Woman and the Girl ascend the dune slowly

Girl — no withering of hope, no canker of the soul ——
Old Woman — no path of pain that we have not trodden, we who walked this place and time before you.
Girl And no path however dark or strange or fearsome we will not walk beside you.
Girl
Old Woman } (*together*) As sure as tide will rise and tide will fall.

Woman It takes courage to walk on into the night. Even more when a lightning bolt reveals that ahead lie pain, decay and loss. But courage is all it takes and in that night, who knows what stars may shine?

The Man is having one of his terrible pressure headaches. He tries to rise onto one knee

Man Help me.
Woman Look. What do you see?

The Man turns to the sea, dizzily, then looks down

Man Broken shells, smashed hopes, forgotten dreams.
Woman We are sand, pressed into rock, hewn into stone, pounded into pebble, washed into shingle, blown into sand. (*She turns to face the Man*)
Old Woman Look again.
Woman We are dust, compacted into bone, strapped into sinew, rising only to fall, tumbling into bone, crumbling into dust. Time and tide washing all away.
Girl Look again.

The Man sweeps the shore DC *with his eyes. He sees something going from* DC *to* UL

Man (*speaking with great difficulty, slurring his words*) Footprints — I think … A row of footprints — stretching —— (*He points* UL)
Old Woman As far as you need to see.

The Man rises, swaying, his balance badly affected, the pain in his head growing

Man I am afraid.

The Girl comes down the DS *side of the dunes*

Girl So much pain past. So much to come.

The Old Woman comes down the US *side of the dunes*

Old Woman Face it.
Girl Embrace it.
Man So alone.
Woman You do not have to walk alone.
Man But they ——
Woman You supported them. Now let them support you.
Man But how? (*He has completely lost his sense of direction. He turns, flailing helplessly*)

The Girl walks in a wide arc DS *of the Man till she is standing* DLC

A lonely seagull calls overhead

Girl No life is ever over. In your body or out of your body, *you* go on.
Old Woman Tide will rise. Tide will fall.

The sound of surf on shingle builds from now to the end of the play

Man I'm — ready.

The Girl and the Old Woman each hold out an arm to him as if to support the Man, but always stay at least an arm's length from him. Slowly the Man seems to sense the direction he must go; during the following he turns to face UL

Woman Use all your skill, however small; all your strength, however weak; all your time, however brief; to place your footprints in the sand.

The Woman begins to hum a lullaby, the same one she sang for the Girl earlier, and begins to back almost imperceptibly away UL. *The other two women join in the lullaby as their lines allow*

The Man begins to take his first steps in the sand, in the direction of
UL. *His gait is unsteady so he holds out his arms to steady himself,*
like a man on a highwire act

The Girl and the Old Woman step in and stand closer to the Man,
but always a step away from him. They are smiling, gently
encouraging, softly urging him on

Old Woman Wind and tide.
Girl Sand and sea.
Man (*seemingly falling, perhaps sinking into the sand*) Help me.

The Old Woman and the Girl take a step in towards the Man

Old Woman Courage. Nothing you face has not been faced before.
Girl Take heart. We are with you, we who walked this path before.
Old Woman Take care. To place your footprint firmly, so those
   who come after you may know which way to tread.
Man They will?
Old Woman As sure as tide will rise ——
Girl — and tide will fall.

The seagull calls. The Man looks up. The pain goes from his face and
he makes his choice

Man Yes. (*Firmly, and with great care, he places his footstep in the*
   sand)

The Old Woman and the Girl freeze. The Woman has almost faded
from our view

The action freezes

The sky glows; sunset. We hear the sounds of sea and surf

Black-out

THE SETTING

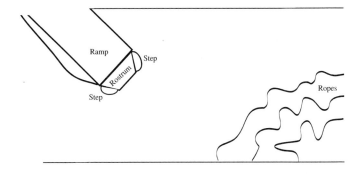

The setting for the original production of this play was as follows: UR a wide, low ramp rose to a small rostrum R of C. From either side of the rostrum a rough step led down to the beach. The ramp, steps and rostrum were sand-coloured. The sea, stretching from DC to LC, was represented by two or three bands of white rope laid in irregular, wavy, but "parallel" lines, suggesting the crests of waves.

FURNITURE AND PROPERTY LIST

On stage: Shells

LIGHTING PLOT

Practical fittings required: nil
Exterior. The same throughout

To open: Mackerel sky on cyclorama; general exterior lighting, predominantly blue and cream. Main light source — the sun — is UL

Cue 1   As the play progresses   (Page 1)
Fade lights slowly on cyclorama, changing from blue and cream to red and yellow

Cue 2   The action freezes   (Page 33)
Bring up glow on cyclorama and stage to indicate sunset

Cue 3   Establish sunset and sounds of sea and surf   (Page 33)
Black-out

EFFECTS PLOT

Cue 1   As play begins   (Page 1)
        Vaughan Williams' "Toward the Unknown
        Region"; surf and seagulls. Fade music
        before action begins; fade surf and seagull
        sounds under opening dialogue

Cue 2   The **Girl** walks DLC   (Page 32)
        Lonely seagull call

Cue 3   **Old Woman**: "Tide will rise. Tide will fall." (Page 32)
        Bring up sound of surf on shingle;
        *   build from now to end of play*

Cue 4   **Girl**: " — and tide will fall."   (Page 33)
        Seagull calls

WARDROBE

Man Casual, modern clothes: a rust or brown short-sleeved shirt, fawn trousers, brown leather sandals.

Woman A long dress, of timeless design, but appropriate to the fifth century, faded to periwinkle blue; bare feet.

Girl A dress of exactly the same design as the Woman's but in a deep blue; bare feet.

Old Woman A fawn dress, poorer than the dresses of the other two women, but of the same period; rust-coloured shawl; bare feet.